The SHAPE of ME and OTHER STUFF

形狀大王國

By Dr. Seuss

文・圖　蘇斯博士
譯　　曾陽晴

形狀大王國　　　　　　　　　　　　　　　　　　　　　蘇斯博士小孩學讀書全集15

發行／1992年12月25日初版1刷　2000年6月25日初版4刷

著／蘇斯博士

譯／曾陽晴

責任編輯／郝廣才　張玲玲　劉思源

美術編輯／李純真　郭倖惠　陳素芳

發行人／王榮文　　出版發行／遠流出版事業股份有限公司　　台北市汀州路3段184號7樓之5

行政院新聞局局版臺業字第1295號　　郵撥／0189456-1　　電話／(02)2365-3707　　傳真／(02)2365-7979

著作權顧問／蕭雄淋律師　　法律顧問／王秀哲律師・董安丹律師

印製／鴻柏印刷事業股份有限公司

YL*ib* 遠流博識網 http://www.ylib.com　　E-mail:ylib@yuanliou.ylib.com.tw

ISBN 957-32-1460-1　　　　　　　　　　　　　　　　　　　　　　　　　　　NT $ 185

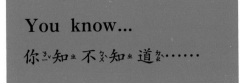

You know...

你³知ㄓ 不ㄅ知ㄓ道ㄉㄠ······

It makes a fellow think.

形ㄒㄧㄥ狀ㄓㄨㄤ可ㄎㄜ以ㄧ讓ㄖㄤ人ㄖㄣ發ㄈㄚ揮ㄏㄨㄟ想ㄒㄧㄤ像ㄒㄧㄤ。

The shape of you

你㲋的㲋形㒼狀㒼

the
shape
of
me

我㲋的㲋形㒼狀㒼

the shape
of everything I see...
我ㄨㄛˇ看ㄎㄢˋ見ㄐㄧㄢˋ的ㄉㄜ˙每ㄇㄟˇ樣ㄧㄤˋ東ㄉㄨㄥ西ㄒㄧ的ㄉㄜ˙形ㄒㄧㄥˊ狀ㄓㄨㄤˋ...

a bug...
小蟲爬

a balloon 汽球大

a bed
床一張

a bike.
腳踏車一輛

No shapes are ever quite alike.

東西各式各樣， 看來並不相像。

Just think about
the shape of beans

想像一一下豆子的形狀

and flowers

花的形狀

and mice

老鼠的形狀

and big machines!

還ㄏㄞˊ有ㄧㄡˇ大ㄉㄚˋ機ㄐㄧ器ㄑㄧˋ的ㄉㄜ˙形ㄒㄧㄥˊ狀ㄓㄨㄤˋ！

Just think about
the shape of strings

想_T像_T一一下_T線_T的_&形_T狀_&

and elephants..

和_&大_&象_T的_&形_T狀_&...

.... and other things.
.... 還ㄏㄞˊ有ㄧㄡˇ其ㄑㄧˊ他ㄊㄚ東ㄉㄨㄥ西ㄒㄧ的ㄉㄜ形ㄒㄧㄥˊ狀ㄓㄨㄤˋ。

The shape of lips.

嘴唇的形狀。

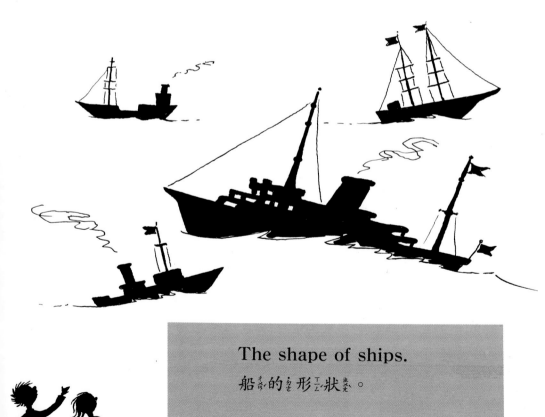

The shape of ships.

船的形狀。

The shape
of water
when
it
drips.

水ㄕㄨㄟˇ滴ㄉㄧ下ㄒㄧㄚˋ來ㄌㄞˊ的ㄉㄜ˙形ㄒㄧㄥˊ狀ㄓㄨㄤˋ。

Peanuts
花生

and 和

pineapples 鳳梨

noses 鼻子

and 和

grapes. 葡萄

Everything

comes

in different shapes.

每ㄇㄟˇ樣ㄧㄤˋ東ㄉㄨㄥ西ㄒㄧ都ㄉㄡ有ㄧㄡˇ各ㄍㄜˋ自ㄗˋ

不ㄅㄨˋ同ㄊㄨㄥˊ的ㄉㄜ˙面ㄇㄧㄢˋ貌ㄇㄠˋ。

Why, George !
You're RIGHT !
哇ㄨㄚ！ 喬ㄑㄧㄠˊ治ㄓˋ！
你ㄋㄧˇ說ㄕㄨㄛ的ㄉㄜ是ㄕˋ！

And...
think about
the shape of GUM !

還ㄏㄞˊ有ㄧㄡˇ……
不ㄅㄨˋ妨ㄈㄤˊ想ㄒㄧㄤ一ㄧ想ㄒㄧㄤ，
口ㄎㄡˇ香ㄒㄧㄤ糖ㄊㄤˊ的ㄉㄜ形ㄒㄧㄥˊ狀ㄓㄨㄤˋ！

The MANY shapes
of chewing gum !

口ㄎㄡˇ香ㄒㄧㄤ糖ㄊㄤˊ嚼ㄐㄧㄠˊ一一嚼ㄐㄧㄠˊ，
形ㄒㄧㄥˊ狀ㄓㄨㄤˋ千ㄑㄧㄢ變ㄅㄧㄢˋ萬ㄨㄢˋ化ㄏㄨㄚˋ真ㄓㄣ不ㄅㄨˋ少ㄕㄠˇ。

And the shape
of smoke
and
marshmallows
and
fires.

還有
煙
和
藥葵
和
火焰。

And mountains　還_{ㄏㄞˊ}有_{ㄧㄡˇ}山_{ㄕㄢ}

and　　和_{ㄏㄢˊ}

roosters　公_{ㄍㄨㄥ}雞_{ㄐㄧ}

and　　和_{ㄏㄢˊ}

horses　　馬_{ㄇㄚˇ}

and　　和_{ㄏㄢˊ}

tires！　輪_{ㄌㄨㄣˊ}胎_{ㄊㄞ}！

And the shape of camels......................

想_{ㄒ一ㄤ}一一_一想_{ㄒ一ㄤ}駱_{ㄌㄨㄛ}駝_{ㄊㄨㄛ}的_{ㄉㄜ}形_{ㄒ一ㄥ}狀_{ㄓㄨㄤ}..................

.... the shape of bees
.... 蜜ㄇㄧ蜂ㄈ的ㄉㄜ形ㄒㄧ狀ㄓㄨㄤ

and the wonderful
shapes of back door keys !
還ㄏㄞ有ㄧㄡ後ㄏㄡ門ㄇㄣ鑰ㄩㄝ匙ㄕ的ㄉㄜ形ㄒㄧ狀ㄓㄨㄤ
奇ㄑㄧ形ㄒㄧ怪ㄍㄨㄞ狀ㄓㄨㄤ非ㄈㄟ常ㄔㄤ棒ㄅㄤ！

**And the shapes
of spider webs**

還有蜘蛛網

and clothes !

和衣服的形狀！

And,
speaking of shapes,
now just suppose... !
還ㄏㄞˊ有ㄧㄡˇ，
講ㄐㄧㄤˇ到ㄉㄠˋ形ㄒㄧㄥˊ狀ㄓㄨㄤˋ，
現ㄒㄧㄢˋ在ㄗㄞˋ讓ㄖㄤˋ我ㄨㄛˇ們ㄇㄣ˙來ㄌㄞˊ假ㄐㄧㄚˇ裝ㄓㄨㄤ……！

Suppose
YOU
were shaped
like these...
假㈠裝㈣
你㈢的㈜
形㈠狀㈣
像㈠這㈣樣㈠……

...or those!
或㈣那㈢樣㈠!

...or shaped
like a BLOGG！
……或者形狀
像個四不像！

Or a garden hose!
或像澆花水管的模樣！

Of all
the shapes
we MIGHT have been...
我ㄨㄛˇ們ㄇㄣˊ可ㄎㄜˇ以ˇ想ㄒㄧㄤˇ像ㄒㄧㄤˋ
自ㄗˋ己ㄐㄧˇ變ㄅㄧㄢˋ成ㄔㄥˊ各ㄍㄜˋ種ㄓㄨㄥˇ形ㄒㄧㄥˊ狀ㄓㄨㄤˋ……

I say, "HOORAY
for the shapes we're in!"
我ㄨㄛˇ說ㄕㄨㄛ：「真ㄓㄣ棒ㄅㄤˋ！
我ㄨㄛˇ們ㄇㄣ˙有ㄧㄡˇ最ㄗㄨㄟˋ好ㄏㄠˇ的ㄉㄜ˙形ㄒㄧㄥˊ狀ㄓㄨㄤˋ！」